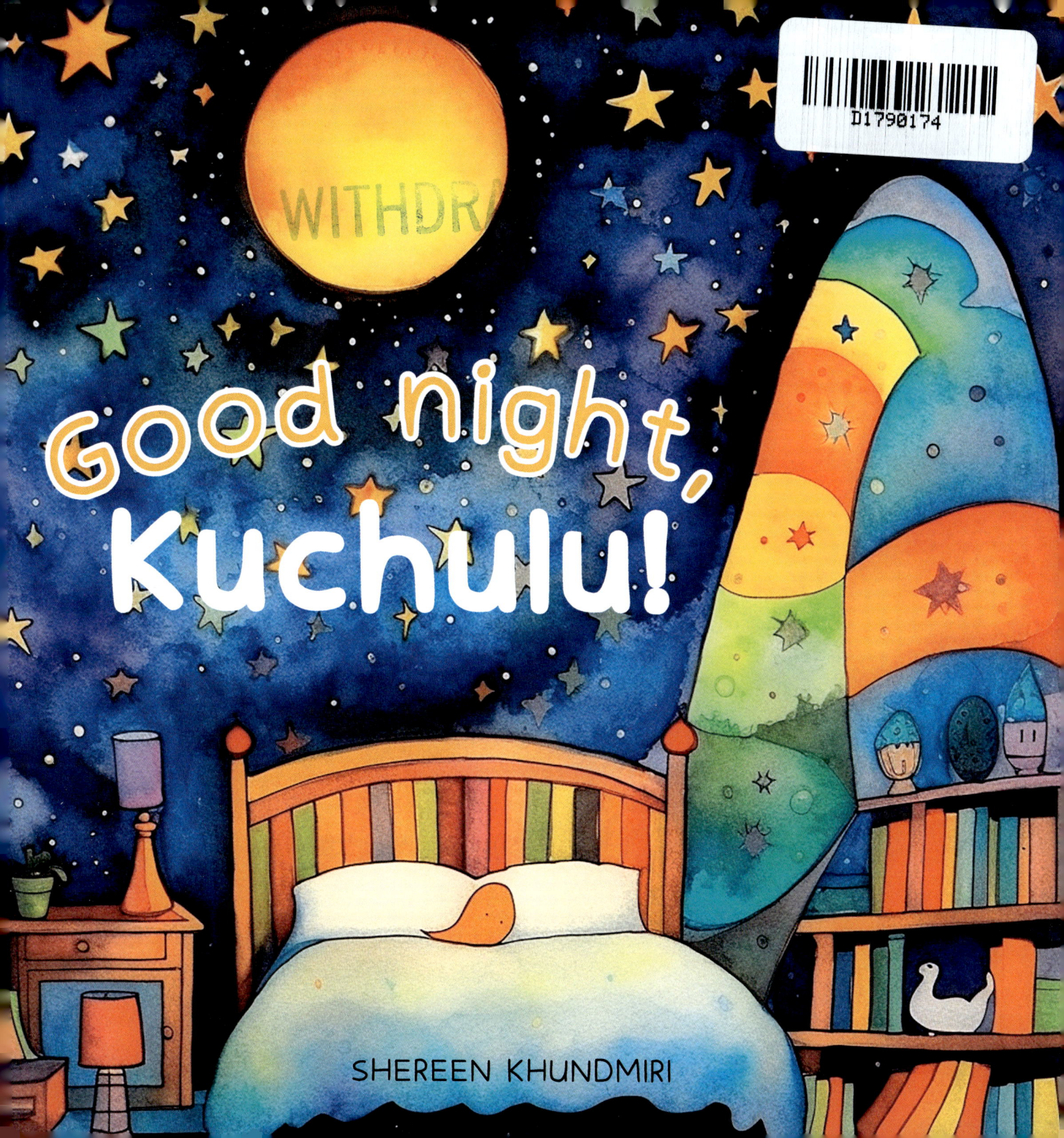

All rights reserved. No part of this publication may be reproduced, distributed, or transmitted in any form or by any means, including photocopying, recording, or other electronic or mechanical methods, without the prior written permission of the publisher, except in the case of brief quotations embodied in critical reviews and certain other noncommercial uses permitted by copyright law.

Copyright © 2023 Shereen Khundmiri

To my dearest treasures, my four shining stars,

This tale of love and hope, spun from our bonds that stretch far.

This story is for you, as the moon is to the night,

A testament of a mother's love, shining ever bright.

May the land of Omeed, guide you when apart,

Just as your love illuminates every corner of my heart.

Shab beKhair, my treasures, under the twinkling skies,

Through every dream and journey, may you always rise.

This book belongs to

_____

Good night, Kuchulu!

SHEREEN KHUNDMIRI

Once upon a time, as the sun began to set, In a world full of colors, where love and hope met.

Lived a playful little one,
Known as Kuchulu, so dear,
With a heart full of dreams,
and not a hint of fear.

"Shab beKhair, Kuchulu," Maman softly says, As the stars started twinkling, ending the day.

But before you close your eyes, under the moon's glow, Let's share a story of a place you should Know.

In the land of 'Omeed' (hope), where dreams take flight, Where the sun always shines, even in the night.

Love, called 'Eshgh', flows like a gentle stream, Filling every heart with a warm, golden gleam.

'Gol' (flowers) of all hues,
dance in a loving trance,
Inviting Kuchulu to join their
harmonious dance.

"Remember Kuchulu," Maman gently spoke, "In Omeed, no heart is ever broke.

For Eshgh is the magic that mends all, Even when you stumble, it won't let you fall."

In the land of Omeed, 'Doost' (friends) are always near, Each one like a 'Setareh' (star), twinkling clear.

The 'Madar Bozorg' (grandmother) owl, wise and kind, And 'Pedar Bozorg' (grandfather) turtle, with a calm mind,

All live in harmony, under the same sky, sending Kuchulu love, as the day goes by.

"Good night, Kuchulu," they all lovingly say, As the moon cast a silvery, calming ray.

And Kuchulu, snuggled up, feeling so light, Whispers, "Shab beKhair," to the soft, tranquil night.

As Maman ends the tale,
under the moon's glow,
She kisses Kuchulu, whispering
words soft and low.

Remember, my Kuchulu, in dreams and in play, Eshgh and Omeed are never far away.

Under the blanket of the star-spangled night,
Kuchulu dreams of Omeed, full of light.

With a heart full of Eshgh,
Kuchulu closed his eyes tight,
Whispering once more...

..."Shab bekhair, good night."

Glossary

little one	Ku•chu•lu	کوچولو
good night	shab•bé•Khair	شب بخیر
mother	mā•mān	مامان
hope	ō•meed	امید
love	éshgh	عشق
birds	par•an•de•gān	پرندگان
garden	bāgh	باغ
flower	gōl	گل
friends	doost	دوست
star	sé•taré	ستاره
baby rabbit	baché•khar•goosh	بچه خرگوش
Kitten	Pi•shi	پی ش
grandmother	mā•mān bō•zōrg	مامان بزرگ
grandfather	ba•ba bō•zōrg	بابا بزرگ

Pronunciation Guide

ā — Sounds like 'o' in the words (short O sound): bop, cop, shop

a — Sounds like 'a' in the words (short A sound): apple, actor, alligator

ō — Sounds like 'o' in the words (long O sound): oval, goat, soap

é — Sounds like 'e' in the words (short E sound): elephant, elegant, egg

kh — Sound comes from the back of the throat

gh — Sound comes from the back of the throat

Made in the USA
Las Vegas, NV
14 March 2025